Samantha Singwell

Written by Penny Robenstone-Harris

Illustrated by Gus Gordon

® sundance™
A Haights Cross Communications ✦® Company

Copyright © 2001 Sundance/Newbridge Educational Publishing, LLC

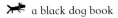 a black dog book

Published by
Sundance Publishing
One Beeman Road
P.O. Box 740
Northborough, MA 01532-0740

Copyright © text Penny Robenstone-Harris
Copyright © illustrations Gus Gordon

First published 2000 by
Pearson Education Australia Pty. Limited
95 Coventry Street
South Melbourne 3205 Australia
Exclusive United States Distribution: Sundance Publishing

Guided Reading Level I
Guided reading levels assigned by Sundance Publishing using the text characteristics
described by Fountas & Pinnell in their book *Guided Reading*, published by Heinemann.

ISBN-13: 978-0-7608-5021-3
ISBN-10: 0-7608-5021-6

Printed in China

Contents

Characters

Samantha wants
to be famous when
she grows up.

Dolores loves
listening to music.

Michael likes to
be in charge of
things.

Chapter One
I Love to Sing

Samantha Singwell loved to sing.

Tra la la. Fa la la la la.

She wondered why her family

was always too busy to listen.

And why did her friend, Dolores,
always go home early when they had
singing practice? But most of all, she
wondered why she never got a part
in the school show.

Samantha's only audience
was her old dog, Rupert.
He was deaf.

The truth was, Samantha couldn't sing.

Dolores tried to tell Samantha.

But Samantha would not listen.

"I'm going to be famous.

I'm going to sing on stage," she said.

Samantha's family raised their eyebrows.

Dolores suggested painting.

But Samantha had another idea.

Chapter Two
Samantha Invites You

"I'm going to put on a show,"
Samantha said.

No one took her seriously.
But Samantha was serious.

She would put on the best show ever.

She practiced in the mirror.

She practiced in the yard.

She even practiced in the shower.

Tra la la. Fa la la.

She sang at breakfast and lunch

and dinner.

Samantha planned her show.

She thought about her friends,

Dolores and Michael,

and how proud they would be.

She decided who she would invite.
She counted the chairs in her house
so everyone would have a seat.

She saved her pocket money
and bought refreshments.

She made invitations on the computer.
Samantha couldn't wait!

Chapter Three
Not a Squeak

Samantha Singwell
invites
__Dolores__
to her special singing show
Saturday 2:00p.m.
at my house

A few days before the show,
Samantha got a funny feeling
in her stomach. She practiced harder.
But now she wasn't sure she sounded like
a famous singer at all.

Dolores and Michael tried to tell her.
"Samantha . . ." they began.

But Samantha had no time to listen.
She had a show to practice for.

On the day of the show,

everyone took a seat.

Samantha was holding her stomach.

"I don't feel well," she said.

"The show must go on!" said Michael.
He flicked on the lights.

"I can't do it!" said Samantha.

"You can!" insisted Dolores,
and she turned on the music.

Everyone stopped talking.

Samantha looked at her audience.

The music grew louder.

Samantha opened her mouth to sing...

There was no sound...

Not even a squeak...

nothing.

Chapter Four
I Love to Dance

Samantha was stunned.

Her mouth tried to make the words

of the song. The audience wriggled.

Samantha began to twitch.

Her feet began to move ... then her arms.

And then her whole body.

The audience began to smile.

"She's dancing!" cried Dolores.

"She's a great dancer!" cried Michael.

The audience jumped up and danced, too.
Samantha's singing was forgotten.

At school the next day,
everyone was talking about
Samantha's dancing.
Mrs. Mars, the music teacher,
invited Samantha to dance in the next
school show.

Samantha was thrilled.

"I'm going to be famous.

I'm going to dance on stage," she said.

"I just love to dance!"